# In the Pines

An 1800s Black / Native American
Novella

# Lisa Shea

Treasure every aspect of yourself.

# In the Pines

# Chapter 1

*Blink.*

Heavy footsteps tromped across the floor, loud curses rang out, and a door slammed shut.

*Blink.*

A tiny hand tugged on her arm. She mumbled that everything was all right.

*Blink.*

Someone somewhere was crying.

*Blink.*

Elizabeth's voice called out in shock. "Sweet Jesus! Naomi!"

*Blink.*

Naomi slowly came awake. The bed beneath her was soft and warm – she knew in an instant that it wasn't hers. She pried her eyes open and looked around in the soft, dusky light. It could have been sunrise, sunset, or a cloudy day – she had no way of telling beyond the closed curtains.

She was in her brother's bedroom – she could see that now. On the opposite wall hung a charcoal drawing of a quiet village in Ireland. Her father had created that a year before he passed away. To her right hung a dreamcatcher – a hoop of willow meant to shield the sleeper from bad dreams. She knew Elizabeth had bought it as a child at a powwow. The talented craftsman had been visiting from the Ojibwe tribe.

Naomi's vision blurred, and she closed her eyes. Her entire body ached; her head felt fuzzy.

*What had happened?*

The door pushed open.

Naomi tensed, pulled her blankets up to her shoulders, and pressed up against the back wall.

Elizabeth eased through the door, her brow creased with worry. Her face gentled as she saw that Naomi was awake. She held a wooden tray with a cornflower-blue pottery bowl on it. The soup's fragrant aroma sent Naomi's stomach rumbling.

Naomi carefully pushed herself up to sitting. She drew in a deep inhale as Elizabeth placed the tray across her lap. The steam was pure ambrosia.

Elizabeth smiled in welcome, taking a seat in the chair at the bed's side. "Johnny and Polly are fine. They're staying in Hiram's room and have been having a grand old time of it. David and William have turned our home into a county fair for the little ones."

Elizabeth took a long swallow of the soup. She was beyond starving; she could feel every movement of the warm liquid down her parched throat. "I'm confused – how long have I been asleep?"

"Two days."

Naomi paused with the spoon midway to her mouth. "Two days?"

Elizabeth nodded. "I found you the afternoon of the twenty-eighth. It's now the thirtieth, in the evening."

Tension snaked through Naomi's body, and she frantically glanced around. "Bill will kill me. He'll absolutely kill me."

Elizabeth shook her head. "Naomi, Bill is gone."

Naomi stared at her. The words didn't quite make sense. They didn't connect together in a way that had meaning.

"I … I don't understand."

Elizabeth leant forward, taking her hand. "Honey, Bill has left town. He must have run off after … whatever happened, happened."

Naomi's hand automatically went to her stomach, to the tiny life that had nestled in there. And somehow, she knew.

God had taken His angel back home.

Her eyes welled with tears, and Elizabeth drew her into her arms, holding her. "I'm so sorry, Naomi. There was nothing I could do. By the time I got there, it was too late."

Sobs shook through Naomi, a culmination of everything that had deluged her these past few days. Strangely, intertwined with the pain and exhaustion came an immense sense of peace. Somehow she had known that her tiny child would only be with her for a short while. Maybe it was the strong sickness – a sickness she had not experienced with either of her other two children. Maybe it was how she teetered on the edge of starvation. She had treasured each day she had, and she knew her child was with God now. Her daughter was safely in a land of peace, love, and plenty.

At last her sobs slowed. She leaned against Elizabeth, drawing in deep breaths.

Elizabeth's hand gently stroked down Naomi's long hair. Her voice was low. "Naomi, did Bill … hit you?"

Naomi shook her head. "He only yanked me, and I was already quite weak. I stumbled and fell. I think …" Her hand moved to her belly. "I think it was just her time. She was a precious jewel. She was too good for this Earth. She belonged in Heaven."

Elizabeth took her hand. "I am sure she will watch over you, and your other two children, as a guardian angel. She will keep you safe from harm."

Naomi glanced at the door, her shoulders tensing. She still couldn't quite believe Elizabeth's news. "You're sure Bill has gone away?"

Elizabeth tilted her head. "You don't seem wholly surprised."

Naomi leant back against the headboard. "He was already making plans to leave. He wanted us to move to somewhere out far west. Mountain-ana, or something like that. Said we had to leave tomorrow." A nervous shudder ran through her shoulders, and she pressed the sensation down with much-practiced effort. "Well, yesterday."

Elizabeth's eyes were wide. "You were going to move away?"

Naomi shook her head. "I said no."

Elizabeth's eyes were saucers now. "You said no to Bill?"

Naomi nodded. "That's why he got upset. And then I ran, and he yanked me, and …"

She looked down at her belly.

Elizabeth took her hand. "We will mourn your child and say prayers for her soul. She will not be forgotten."

Naomi made the effort to bring a smile onto her lips. "Thank you. I could not have asked for a better sister."

Elizabeth gave her hand a squeeze. "And now we need to nurse you back to health. If I had to guess, you've been living on air and vapors these past few months. So let's start with this soup. One step at a time."

Naomi nodded and picked up her spoon. Every slurp seemed more delicious than the last, and she was comfortably full by the time the bowl was empty.

Elizabeth took up the tray. "Are you ready to see your children now? Or would you like to rest for a bit first?"

For the first time in many days, an authentic smile came to Naomi's lips. "My children are my life. They will renew me more than any amount of rest could."

Elizabeth nodded. "I thought you might say that. I'll be right back."

There were descending footsteps, a pause, and then a thundering of little feet as Johnny came scrambling up. He launched himself at his mother, a tiny, dark blur with dense, curly hair. He buried his head into his mother's chest. "Mama!"

Elizabeth stepped in, Polly in her arms, and she laid the toddler against Naomi's other side.

Tears welled in Naomi's eyes as she drew the two tiny, warm bodies against her own. Her precious children were safe. Against all odds, against all that life had stacked up against them, they were finally safe. Bill had fled to escape the wrath of the Carter brothers. She fervently prayed that Bill was somewhere across the Mississippi by now. Who knew, maybe this was what he'd wanted all along – to be free of the dark-skinned family he'd created and to be able to start fresh with someone "better."

Naomi looked down at her two darling angels, their skin the color of light coffee, their curly hair framing their faces. They were the most beautiful children she'd ever seen.

Johnny's eyes shone with delight. "Mama! Mama! We had chicken and apples! Grilled pumpkin seed and roasted pecans! And Polly here tried mashed pears! She loved them!"

Naomi kissed Polly's forehead. "My, aren't you a big girl now!"

Elizabeth gave a wry smile. "I hope you don't mind. We had to feed her something, and –"

Naomi blushed. "I understand. And, really, I should have started weaning her already. It's just, with the food we had …" She looked down.

"I know, Naomi. You did the best you could. It's all any of us can do."

Johnny looked up at Naomi. "Mama, is Papa coming back?"

Naomi's shoulders tightened. She looked down into the large, innocent eyes of her son. She swallowed, then said, truthfully, "I don't know, Johnny. I think he might have gone west, on a trip."

Johnny looked at his younger sister, then back at his mother. "I hope his trip takes a long, long time. He was always so angry. It made my stomach hurt."

Naomi drew him in. "I'm so sorry, sweetie. You were brave, so brave, to deal with everything."

He snuggled against her. "I'm just glad you're ok, Mama." He looked up at her. "Are you ok?"

She looked between her two children and her eyes shone.

"Yes, sweetheart. Everything will be all right."

# Chapter 2

*Bill was holding her by her shoulders, furiously shaking her, his eyes bulging from their sockets.*

*"Where did you go! You damned crow half-breed! You Mick injun whore! Why weren't you home when I came back! Where were you?"*

*Naomi fought to speak, but her throat was closing ... closing ... She couldn't breathe ...*

Naomi blinked awake in the streaming morning sunlight, her heart thundering against her chest. Polly and Johnny were snuggled in close against her, the thick covers over all three of them.

There was not a sound in the house.

She drew in deep breaths, willing herself to calm, reciting the mantra that she was safe now.

Slowly, steadily, her breathing returned to normal.

She pressed a tender kiss to each of her child's foreheads. She closed her eyes for a long moment, sending a heartfelt thanks to God for all the blessings she had. There was so much to be grateful for.

Then she gently wriggled past the two children, tucking them back into their hollows, before going to the door. She was dressed in a thick, flannel nightgown in blue check which covered her from neck to floor. Her sister-in-law's, undoubtedly. There was a dark blue robe hanging on the black of the door and she drew it on. Then she headed down the stairs.

David was sitting at the kitchen table.

She soaked in the sight of him. So much had happened, these past few days. The last she had seen him, he had risked his life fighting against the Carter brothers, all odds against him, in order to keep her safe.

Now he sat in the morning sun, his amber eyes on hers, his skin the color of freshly tilled earth. His dark curls hung around his face, framing it. She could see the firm muscles beneath his blue shirt, the strength in his hands - but it was the resolve in his eyes that held her.

She knew, if Bill tried to return and hurt her or her family, that David would stand by her. No matter what it took, he would be there at her side.

Her throat went dry.

David's eyes held hers, and a smile eased on his face. "It's good to see you up, Naomi. Lizzie's attentive nursin' has done some good. Would you like some coffee? It's fresh."

Her stomach flitted with butterflies. It was all she could do to draw a breath and nod. She pointed at the back door. "I just have to –"

His grin grew. "Take your time. I'll be waiting when you get back."

She took care of her business faster than she'd ever before. The world around her glistened gold and silver in the morning sunlight, as if the world had been gilded just for her.

True to his world, David had a second dark brown, glazed pottery mug across from his by the time she returned. Alongside the steaming coffee was a thick slice of fresh bread slathered with raspberry jam.

Her mouth watered.

She eased into the seat opposite him, taking a long drink of the fragrant liquid, then a bite of the warm bread. Her eyes closed in delight. She couldn't remember when she had last eaten this well.

David watched her quietly, taking a sip of his own coffee. His voice rumbled out of him, low and soothing. "The children have been darlings. They've loved spending time with their cousin. You should take your time to heal up. You've been through a lot."

She nodded. "I couldn't have done it without God's support. Pastor Smith's sermon today will have even more meaning for me than usual."

His brows creased with concern. "Are you sure you're up for it? You've been through quite a lot, and you're barely out of bed. I'm sure the Pastor would be happy to come by after service to talk privately with you."

She shook her head. "The Good Lord has brought me to this place of safety. All I have to do in return is walk the few steps to sit in His holy place and show my appreciation for all He has done."

"If that is your wish, then I will help however I can."

She could feel her cheeks tint. "Thank you. I appreciate it."

Her chest constricted, and she looked into those eyes. "I never said thank you for saving my life. For saving all of our lives. If you and William hadn't come through that door –"

He put his hand out over hers, and a wave of contentment swept through her.

*Everything would be all right.*

His gaze was steady, serious, and went to her soul. "I would do it again in a heartbeat. I am just grateful we were in time."

How could his hands be both so strong and so gentle?

A noise sounded from behind them, and they pulled their hands apart with a start. Elizabeth stumbled sleepily down the stairs followed by William. Her eyes lit up when she saw Naomi and David at the table. "Ah, you're up! I had hoped you might sleep in another day or two."

David nudged his head at Naomi. "She wants to go to service this morning."

Elizabeth's head swiveled to look at Naomi. "Sweetie, are you sure? You don't need to go."

Naomi smiled at her. "I know. I want to. I'll be fine."

"All right, then. I've got a number of dresses for you to choose from – I'm sure they'll all fit plumb right. And we can get the children ready in no time."

Naomi bit her lip. She wanted to ask about her own dress, but she had a feeling that it was beyond repair. And she didn't want to have to admit to them that that one dress was all she owned. Not counting the light, summer dress that she had cut apart in order to make Johnny his Christmas present.

Elizabeth must have seen something of the worry in Naomi's eyes, for she came over to wrap a fond arm around her. "Cuz, we're all family here. We all help each other." She nudged her head at David. "When David was young, he broke his leg fallin' from a tree. Our father carried him

ten miles to a doctor, to get it set. Now that our
father is older, David's been taking care of him.
Cooking his meals and such. It's what family
does. We watch over each other and love each
other."

Naomi looked to David, her heart warming.
How many sons would put aside their own lives to
take such good care of a parent? David had a
strong sense of loyalty, and he showed it through
his actions, rather than words.

A cold flush ran through her, and she looked
down. He was caring for his father – and he was
only here in Tennessee on a short visit. Soon he
would be returning to North Carolina, to the
Oxendines.

And she would be left behind.

She took another drink of her coffee, forcing a
smile on her lips. Whatever God had for her, she
would find a way to accept it. He had already
worked the greatest miracle she could ask for.

There were thundering footsteps above, and
soon the morning was a whirl of laughing
children, smiling adults, and the rounds of
washing and cleaning which came before a
Sunday service. It seemed all too soon that they
were walking in a merry mob along the town's
main street toward the church. Elizabeth carried
Polly, bouncing her along, and Naomi took in
each sight as if the world were brand new.

A flock of juncos hopped the porch in front of the general store, pecking at stray grain. A horse whinnied from the small barn behind the Pastor's home. Bright sunshine sparkled along the snow, creating a beautiful send-off for 1809. Naomi wondered what the next decade of the nineteenth century would bring. She would pray for this new country of hers, to bring it to a place of equality and serenity.

Pastor Smith was standing at the doorway, greeting each person in turn. He beamed as he saw Naomi approaching with her family. When she came to a stop before him, he put out his arms and drew her into a warm hug.

"My child. My sweet, dear child. I am so glad to see you up and on your feet."

He drew back from her, and his aged brow creased. His voice dropped lower. "I am so, so sorry for your loss."

She nodded. "Thank you, Pastor."

She followed her brother in, and they slid into their pew. The two young cousins giggled, nudging each other over who knew what joke.

Then David slid in at her other side.

It seemed hardly possible. It was barely a week since she first saw David at the Christmas service. And here she was, six days later, and she owed her life to him. Her own life – and that of her two small children.

She had prayed to God, in this very pew, and asked for His help. She had placed herself into His tender care.

And now all that she could have hoped for had come true.

She bowed her head in complete gratitude.

The congregation shuffled in, the sun glistened through the large windows, and at last Pastor Smith came down the aisle to his position at the front of his flock. His sermon was rich with song and love, with stories and sharing.

Then he turned to the gathered and smiled at them. "This year of ours, 1809, has seen many changes. This was the year that our third president, Thomas Jefferson, ended his eight years of service ruling our new country. He performed many great acts. It is thanks to him that we acquired the Louisiana Purchase and doubled the size of our lands. He sent out Louis and Clark to explore those new stretches of wilderness. In 1803, President Jefferson brought us a brand-new state, Ohio."

The Pastor's face shadowed. "Our president was not always concerned with all under his watch, though. I have a friend who works high-up in our government. It appears that Jefferson has made a number of statements promoting the removal of all those with Indian blood to locations west of the Mississippi."

William's brow creased with concern, and he spoke up. "But our families have lived on these lands for thousands of years. We know every tree – we understand every twist in the Blackburn Fork. What would we do in the flat, grassy plains of the West?"

Pastor Smith nodded. "Luckily, we now have James Madison as our president, and we can pray that he understands the needs of all residents of this great land of ours. With effort, we can find a way to live in harmony and peace."

He looked across the room. "As you know, relations have become tense with Britain. In Madison's State of the Union in November, he discussed the preparations for going back to war against them."

There were mutters around the room. William spoke up again. "We have barely recovered from the last war. I would not like to see those hardships visited on our own children." His hand rested gently on Hiram's shoulder.

"We all would like to avoid war," agreed the Pastor. "But Britain's Orders in Council is blocking a substantial amount of our trade. It makes impossible for us to get the goods we need – and to sell the goods we produce here. We have to convince them to rescind those orders."

Naomi looked down at her two small children. These issues between governments seemed far away to her. All she needed was some line to catch fish, some cloth to make clothes from, and a safe home. She wished that life could be simpler.

She looked between her brother and David. If war came again to her land, the two men could easily be sucked away in it. Sucked away – and never to return again.

The shadowed thought twisted around her as the sermon came to a close, as they rose and headed out into the crisp, sunny December air. She looked to David. "You don't think there'll really be war, do you?"

His eyes held hers. "I hope not. But the Pastor is right. Our country can't survive if we're forced to live on our own. Our world is too interconnected. We need other countries – and they need us. We have to find a way to make this work."

Naomi shook her head, running a hand through her hair. "If only we could all just get along with each other."

He gave a wry smile. "If only."

He looked up – and stopped. He shifted so his body was in front of Naomi.

Naomi blinked, looking ahead.

Coming at them down the snowy street, four abreast, were the Carter brothers.

# Chapter 3

As if from a great distance Naomi heard Elizabeth's shriek of alarm; she knew that Elizabeth had gathered up the three children in a tense huddle. William strode forward to join David; both men stood balanced on the balls of their toes, their hands loose at their sides.

Naomi's heart threatened to pound clear out of her chest. This had to be a nightmare. It could not be the four Carter brothers striding down the street toward her. But there was Jim's dark eyes and Richard's bandaged face. All of them were far worse for the wear from the last time they'd approached her. There were dark, angry bruises and jagged, blood-edged scars. Todd was smeared with gooey ointments, but it was clear that he was suffering from severe burns. He limped as he moved closer.

The brothers drew to a stop about five feet from the two men.

Jim coughed. "We've come … that is, we're here …"

Naomi was poised on the edge of flight. She'd grab her children, flee …

David shifted, his eyes moving …

A small, dark woman pushed her way from between Jim and Todd. She seemed to be in her fifties, her dark skin crackled with lines, her hair specked with grey. She wore a faded blue dress with large, rust-colored spots on it.

She whacked Jim hard on his stomach. He must have been wounded there – he winced hard and nearly doubled over.

Her voice was the cawing of a crow. "Speak it up. It's cold out, and the woman don't have all day."

Jim groaned. "Yes, Ma."

Naomi's gaze went more attentively between the woman and the four men near her. Yes, she could see it now. The way their brows bushed together. The sharp slant of their noses. They were all related.

Jim looked past David and William to Naomi. "Naomi, we're … um … sorry. Sorry we might'a hurt you a few nights ago. We was just liquored up, with what Bill had done to Richard and all."

Richard's eyes glowed. "Yeah, if that bastard hadn't started it, by punching me in the –"

His mother turned and hit him – hard – in the face. His shriek could be heard clear to the Blackburn Fork.

His cry mangled into words. "Ma! Why did ya do that?"

His mother's mouth twisted into a frown. "I done told ya to apologize, not to make excuses." She raised a hand. "Now don't make me hit you again."

"Yes, Ma. I'm sorry, Ma." He turned to Naomi. "I'm done sorry, too. Warn't your fault that Devil Bill is a no-good two-timing whore-mongering –"

His mother's hand twitched.

He winced at the threat and pressed his lips shut tight.

Todd nodded, his face creased in pain. Naomi could see the sharp agony that accompanied every movement he made. His voice was a hoarse rasp. "I'm done sorry. Lord knows I'm being punished for what I did."

The woman turned on Sam, her eyes sharp.

Sam's face was dark, but after a moment under his mother's gaze he wilted. "Yeah, I'm sorry, too. Guess'n you had enough to deal with from Bill, wit'out us coming after you, too."

The mother crossed her arms under her breasts and turned to look at Naomi. "My boys'r gonna make amends to you. For what they done."

Naomi looked across the four wounded men. Her throat closed up. "That's not really neccess-"

The woman's eyes sharpened. "I said they's gonna make amends, and that's what they's a gonna do."

Naomi retreated back within herself. No wonder that woman managed to keep her four sons under her thumb even though they outweighed her by two hundred pounds each. She was a force of nature.

David's voice was low. "What did you have in mind, Mrs. Carter?"

The woman spat. "Miss," she corrected. "The bastard who done spawned these four took off on us just after Richard here was born. I had to raise them on my own. Took a strong hand, and a barrel-full of switches, but we made it through."

"Miss Carter," amended David.

"We done went out to Bill's place, yesterday, to apologize in person, but she warn't there. And I saw the hell-hole he was keeping her in." Her mouth turned down. "Lucky you all didn't freeze to death at the first snap."

Naomi wrapped her arms around herself. She could just about die from embarrassment, to have that woman there feeling pity for *her*. It wasn't like Naomi was *in the pines*, better than anyone else. But, still, her family had always prided themselves on helping others and living by the Bible's rules. Clearly the men in front of her had a different interpretation of proper living. And now they were pitying *her*?

David's voice cut into her musings. "So, Miss Carter, how did you propose to make up to Naomi what you put her through?"

Miss Carter poked a finger at Jim. "Jim and the boys are a-gonna built her a new house."

Naomi blinked. "What?"

Miss Carter nodded. "A proper house, here in town. I done heard that Bill ran off, skittered like a possum with his tail a'tween his legs, just like my slack-jawed man did." She spat on the ground. "Men. Can't trust a-one of 'em."

Her dark eyes came up to stare into Naomi's. "So ya don't need ta live out in that tiny monk's cell any more. You can come live with your kin." She nudged her head at the children huddling behind Elizabeth. "Best, to help you raise your two dibs. Have family 'round."

Her voice dropped to a mutter. "Wish I had family 'round, when my man ran off. I's just left on my own."

Naomi shook her head. "I don't know, it doesn't –"

William turned to her. His voice held true curiosity. "Do you want to stay out in the woods in that house?"

She stared at him. The thought that she could leave that location had simply never occurred to her. That was where Bill had taken her. That is where Bill told her to stay. So she stayed.

And now Bill was gone.

A glowing, bright spirit lit within her, lifting her up.

David turned, and for a moment his breath caught. He simply stared at her. Then he found his voice. "Naomi, what do you want to do?"

She looked between the two men, then over to the short woman who waited beyond.

Naomi nodded, a joyful warmth radiating from her core. "I would like very much to live in town."

Miss Carter turned to Jim. "Ya hear that, Jim? You and your brothers will be here at dawn tomorrow morning – and every morning after that – until this house is done. I don't care if it takes two weeks. You'll build her a proper house. Two bedrooms. Fireplace. You hear me?"

Jim nodded his head in full acceptance.

Her brow furrowed. "Then, when's the house is done, you and your lot are going out to work for my brother, in the west. Time you had a proper man in your life, to beat some sense into you."

The four men's eyes dropped to their shoes in submission.

William turned to Miss Carter. "David and I will help with the construction. I'll get the hardware and glass for the windows. We'll make a log cabin, to get it up quickly. It's winter, after all, and the weather could turn nasty at any point.

"Fine." Miss Carter moved her eyes to hold Naomi's. "So, we're square?"

Naomi's eyes moved across the four men. They would have raped her, had William and David not stormed in to rescue her.

But the alternative was to call in the law and drag the community through a trial. Subject her children to life-long notoriety.

She couldn't do that to them.

She nodded. "We're square."

There was almost a hint of a smile on Miss Carter's lips. "You're a strong woman, Naomi. Bill's takin' off was the best thing that ever could'a happened to you. Don't you forget it."

Naomi felt a connection between her and the wrinkled woman before her.

*There, but for the grace of God ...*

"I won't forget it."

The woman spun on her heel. The four men trailed after her, four whipped dogs limping with their tails between their legs.

David turned to William with a raised eyebrow. "That was unexpected."

William nodded, then looked up at the sun's position, sliding along its path in the sky. "And it means we gotta get busy, if we're going to be ready for the morning.

David waved a hand. "After you!"

The two men headed off at a fast stride toward the general store.

Elizabeth came up to Naomi, her face pale with relief. "Thank goodness, you'll be near us. I was worried about you being out in that cabin all on your own with the two little cooter cats. Now we'll be neighbors!"

Naomi looked down at Polly, Johnny, and Hiram. At how they clumped together like raisins in a bowl, all alike, all looking at her with bright hope in their eyes.

Johnny spoke first. "Really, Mama? We'll get to live next to Auntie Elizabeth and Uncle William? Liketa one big family?"

She dropped to a knee and drew him into a warm hug.

"Yes, sweetheart. One big, joyful, happy family."

# Chapter 4

The children were all long asleep by the time William and David brought home the last of the supplies. Elizabeth had hot cider waiting for them in heavy pottery mugs, along with a fresh pone of bread all ready for buttering. The four adults took chairs around the crackling fire.

William smiled at Naomi. "Everything's ready for the morning, Naomi. That land to our left is nice and flat – we've been using it to grow corn but we can easily do that further out. We got the basic supplies we need, and Mr. Lowery has sent a rider with an order to bring in the window glass and other items within a few days."

David nodded. "Luckily, we don't need any nails for this. With the way log homes settle, they'd just twist any nails out along the way. The weight of the logs – and the cross-hatching – holds them in place."

Naomi looked across the other three. "It still feels so unreal. Like I'm dreaming. I can't believe how much my life has changed in the past week."

Elizabeth smiled. "You deserve it, Naomi, you poor creeter. You've been through so much, and you hung in there every day. You never lost your faith."

She raised her mug. "A toast. To Naomi. We have a new year. A new start. A new lease on life."

Four mugs met together in the middle, and Naomi glowed with joy. This was really happening. It wasn't a dream. Tomorrow morning a new house would begin to appear out of scratch, rising from the ashes.

Naomi looked at the three sitting near the fire. "I don't know how to thank you all. You've made my dreams come true."

William patted her arm. "We'll always be here for you, little sis."

A loud yawn erupted from Naomi, and Elizabeth smiled. "All right, you've had a long day, and you need to rest up. Go on up to bed – get some sleep."

Naomi flushed. "I can't take your bedroom. Not again."

Elizabeth chuckled. "I thought you might say that. So we put Hiram into our bed, and we'll be sleeping with him tonight. You can sleep in the other room with your two darling tykes."

Naomi looked to David. "But where will you sleep?"

He smiled and looked to the fire. "Right here. Believe me, it's toasty warm, and it's far better than many other places I've slept over the years. I'm quite fine."

Naomi finished her cider, then stood. "I'll wish you all a good night, then, and I'll see you in the morning."

Elizabeth smiled at her. "Sleep well, Naomi."

Naomi looked across the three, her heart glowing with joy. She ended with David, and then turned.

The warmth of his gaze stayed with her all the way up the stairs.

Lisa Shea

# Chapter 5

Gentle dawn sunlight streamed across the wooden floor of the living room, dancing a trail against the polished planks. Naomi sat with the other adults at the kitchen table, her heart thundering against her ribs. Somehow she was deluged with a mixture of anticipation, fear, and perhaps even a tinge of panic.

*If Bill were to come back ...*

A knock came on the front door, and four pairs of heads turned from the table. David and William got up, moving through the golden shadows while Naomi remained next to Elizabeth, the steaming coffee in front of them forgotten.

Naomi willed her thundering heart to slow. If it had been Bill, he wouldn't have knocked. He would have simply kicked the door down.

William glanced at David before pulling open the door.

The four Carter brothers stood there before them, bundled up against the chill, their faces solemn. Jim nodded to William. "We're here, as agreed. We'll do whatever it takes to get Naomi's house built."

William pulled on his coat and boots, and David did the same. Then the six men headed next door into the open field.

A thrill of nervous tension swept through Naomi, and she ran across the floor, pulling on her own gear in mere minutes. Then she stepped out into the drifting snow.

The sun peeked over the trees. Waves of warm light flooded across the small village.

Naomi's heart was swept away. It was really happening. There the six men were, striding across the land, motioning to small furrows here or a smoother spot there. Behind her, from the second floor, she could hear the excited squeals of the children as they peered out the window. No doubt in a few minutes there would be tiny bundles of joy making snow angels or lobbing snowballs.

But right now – for this one moment – there was that powerful sense of anticipation. The beauty of a blank slate. The sense that anything at all could happen and she was here to witness it.

Her faith and suffering had, at last, been rewarded.

There was a movement at her side and she flinched, pulling in against herself. She turned …

Elizabeth came to stand next to her, gently patting Naomi on the shoulder. "A good day to begin anew," murmured Elizabeth. Her eyes twinkled. "I bet the kids down their breakfast in ten seconds flat."

Naomi shook off her shadows. "I'm surprised they're stopping for breakfast at all." Her eyes sparkled. "But it'd be hard for anyone to resist those cinnamon rolls you make."

Elizabeth wrapped her arm around Naomi's side, then murmured in her ear, "You know, it's all because you said no."

Naomi blinked. "What do you mean?"

"To Bill. You could have said yes. You could, right at this very moment, be tromping through the snow, carrying your two tiny children, and you could have collapsed on the trail. He could have left you there to die. And your path in life could have been very different."

Naomi blinked. Elizabeth was right. God had given her blessings, certainly. He had always been there to lend support. But she had to take that step. She had to demonstrate her dedication to her family. If she had lost strength – had gone along with Bill's demands …

She shivered.

Her hands ran along her coat, and she thought again of that fateful night. She had still been wearing David's shirt, when the confrontation had taken place. That small token had emboldened her – had reminded her that there were those who cared for her. Who were willing to stand by her, if she only gave them that chance.

She wondered how many other women were out there, needing a friend, needing that one tiny token to get them through to the other side.

There was a chorus of delighted cheers from behind them, and three little forms came tumbling into the snow. Naomi swooped up Polly from Johnny's arms and drew her close. Naomi pointed to the lot. "Sweetie, that's where our house will be."

Polly scrunched up her face and stared at the empty space.

Naomi pressed a kiss on her daughter's forehead. It was a dream. A glorious, wonderful dream.

The day spun by in chopping trees and dragging logs. The snow made much of the task easy – the logs practically slid by themselves from the forest over to the lot. Jeff, the owner of the general store, came by to lend a hand, leaving his wife and young daughter to look over the counter. Jeff's draught horse made easy work of gathering the large logs.

The men broke for lunch, sitting in the center of a ring of logs to have warm cider and chicken jerky. Then it was back to notching the ends of the logs and carefully stacking them. One layer, then the next. By the time the sun was easing below the horizon they had the structure frame a good ten logs high.

Jim nodded to William. "We'll be back at dawn."

William nodded. "You did good work."

Jim blinked in surprise, then an almost-smile hinted on his lips. He turned with his brothers, and they faded into the shadows of the forest.

Jeff came over. "They're rough lads, no doubt about it, but I think there's good hidden in there as well. Zilla's brother will be able to carve them into shape. It'll just take him some time."

William looked at him. "You know the brother?

Jeff nodded. "Sure thing – he grew up around here. A tough man, but well grounded. He's a no-nonsense sheriff out there in the west. He'll drive those boys hard, but he'll make them into men. Make them earn every step of the way."

David looked into the shadows. "Sounds like what they need. If we hadn't been there, when they took Naomi …" His gaze hardened.

Jeff nodded. "And they'll pay for that. For years. It's a lesson they'll learn well."

Naomi flushed, hearing the men talk about that night. David was right, of course. She had been teetering on the edge of an event which would have scarred her forever. The Carter brothers would have to perform years of penance before she felt they had made up for that.

But, listening to Jeff, she had a sense that that was exactly what waited for them. And, deep within her, she did also harbor a sense that every person deserved a second chance. Even for a heinous act, they deserved an opportunity to do whatever punishment was set out and to rise above their past choices.

She hoped the Carter brothers would finish that journey.

Jeff shook hands with the other two men. "Well, time for me to get home to my family. I'll see you both tomorrow?"

William smiled. "You don't have to, really. The four brothers are hard workers and are attentive to what they're doing. Whatever else their mother might have done or not done, she drilled that into them."

"I don't mind," assured Jeff. "It's quiet this time of year, now that the holidays are done with. People are hunkering down at home and mending. It'll be another few months before they start buying the supplies for spring. So I'm happy to help."

He glanced up at the sky. "Besides, one never knows if the weather will hold. So we should get the house up as quickly as we can, in case a storm blows in."

"Well, then, we appreciate it."

Jeff headed down the street to his own home, located on the far side of his store. Then David and William came to accompany Naomi into the house.

David smiled at Naomi as they all climbed out of their boots and jackets. "So, what do you think so far?"

"It's hard to even express it," she murmured. "I'd never dreamed of having a house as fine as this, all my own. To have it springing up out of nothing is a right miracle. I don't know how I can repay you all."

Elizabeth smiled from her spot by the fire. "You can repay us by getting back to full strength. Come on, the pumpkin seed stew is ready."

The family piled around the table, and Polly's little arms reached eagerly for the mashed pears.

Naomi beamed with joy. A short week ago she never could have dreamed such a scene could happen. It would have seemed beyond fantastic. And here she was, cozily warm, a plate of delicious food and a mug of warm cider at her fingertips.

Elizabeth twined her fingers together, and the rest of the family followed suit. Elizabeth's voice was warm. "Thank you, oh Lord, for the blessings you've brought to us today. Thank you for the food on our table, the roof over our head, and the warmth of our kin. Thank you for the good weather to build Naomi's house and the helpful assistance of others. Amen."

"Amen," echoed the other voices. And then the feast began.

Naomi was sure that her stomach had reached the size of a full-term pregnancy by the time she carried Polly upstairs to bed. Johnny's yawn nearly split his small head, and she smiled fondly at the boy. The children were settling in well to this new life. She could see the life in his eyes, the spring in his step which had been missing before.

He climbed up into bed, and she gently lay his sister next to him. Usually he would be begging for a story – but not tonight. His eyes were closed by the time his curly head touched the pillow.

The other three adults were sitting around the crackling fire as she came down, and she took a minute to look at them from the stairs. They weren't *in the pines* by any stretch of the imagination. They wore simple clothes. The room had just the straight-backed chairs and a low, wooden table. The mantle over the fireplace held a trio of carvings of wood ducks.

But each item in here was made with care and love. Elizabeth's seam-work was beyond compare. William's woodwork and carving shone with an attention to detail.

She took her seat by the fire, and a basking warmth shimmered through her. A sense of peace. Contentment. It was all so new to her that she took a long moment just to soak it in. She had felt like this, long ago, when she was young. Before she had met Bill. Her father and mother had nurtured a house full of love and laughter. His Irish lilt and her bright giggle …

But then her father had passed away, when she was not even ten, and some of the joy had gone out of the home. Her mother had smiled less. And then William had met Elizabeth, and moved away, and somehow the gloom had settled further.

When Naomi had seen Bill, that fateful day, he had seemed an escape from all of that. But Naomi could see now how wrong that had been. She hadn't needed an escape. One could never escape from who they were. She needed to find, within herself, that desire for joy. And then she needed to find a man worthy to stand by her side and share in that.

Her eyes rose to meet David's.

She smiled.

# Chapter 6

Tuesday … Wednesday … Thursday … the house climbed toward the Heavens. A second floor appeared, and the men were up on ladders, heaving the heavy logs up through a system of ropes and pulleys. Jeff's horse did his part, as did Pastor Smith's gentler mare. Pastor Smith was too elderly to lend a hand directly, but he did offer encouragement and keep an eye on the little ones while Elizabeth and Naomi shuttled supplies and coffee to the workers.

By Friday the men were laying down the roofing while the women worked inside at sealing the cracks between the logs. Jeff's wife, Amanda, came over to lend a hand. She was a portly woman with a wide smile and thick, dark hair. Their six-year-old daughter, Jessica, was a mirror image of her mother.

Hiram came skipping in the door, his gaze attached firmly on Jessica. "You must be hungry. Come have a roll. We've got dill butter!"

Jessica's eyes went round, and she looked at her mother. "Oh, could I?"

Amanda smiled. "Of course. You've been a wonderful help. Go on and get some food into you."

The two kids scampered off through the open door.

Amanda chuckled, looking over at Elizabeth. "I do think your son has a crush on my Jessica. Every time you come to the store, he finds a way to spend the time talking with her."

Elizabeth smiled. "Plenty of time for those two."

Amanda grinned. "It goes by in the blink of an eye, it does. You'll look twice and they'll be at that church, holding hands and walking up the aisle, man and wife."

Elizabeth smiled. "Seems like only yesterday that that was me. But it's been ten years! I definitely treasure every moment I have with Hiram. I know it'll seem all too soon that he'll be off and with a family of his own. And who knows if they'll stay close or move away."

Naomi looked at Elizabeth. "Do you miss your own family?"

Elizabeth gave a soft shrug. "At times I do. My father could be a little rough, but he had his tender moments as well. But would I want to move down to South Carolina?"

She shook her head. "There's a sickness coming to our land. Used to be, we all worked together. Black, white, Indian, we were all simply people. We struggled in the winter and farmed in the summer. But now …"

She shrugged. "Now, it seems the whites want to lay claim on everything they see. Lay claim on the blacks and use them as slaves. Lay claim to the lands and push out the Indians who owned it. And that sentiment seems to be worse down south. Up here in Tennessee, at least, there's still some sense of each person holding their own. That nature's enough of a threat without us turning on each other."

She looked through the open window at her own house. "If I could, I've move even further north with Hiram. Somewhere I felt safe. And I'd move my father up here to live with us. His tongue could always be a little too quick for his own good. It could get him into trouble."

She shrugged. "But he's where he is and he doesn't want to move. He likes it here. Has friends and family. So he's determined to stick it out, no matter what."

She looked around. "And, I have to admit, I like it here. I like Pastor Smith's sermons. I like my friends. I like the quiet lifestyle we live. If I moved us north – to Pennsylvania or even New York – what if it wasn't any better? What if it was worse?" She drew her coat tighter around her. "And of course, I think it's quite cold enough where we are now. Do I really want to go even further north?"

Naomi grinned. "You might think about it come summertime again. I remember last summer, when the skeeters were as big as bats!"

Elizabeth laughed. "That's for sure. But skeeters can be wrangled with. The cold? It's much harder to bear." She nodded. "No, I'm happy here. This is where we've set down roots, and this is where we'll stay. Hopefully the president will get a handle on these changes and set things right. After all, we're a new country. We're still figuring these things out."

Naomi sighed. "I hope you're right."

There was a tromping from above, a shaking of a ladder, and William poked his head in the front doorway. "Well, that's it for the roof. The sun's heading down, so we'll put off the finishing work until tomorrow. We'll get the doors on, the windows in, and then it'll be set! You'll be all ready to spend your first night in your very own home!"

Naomi looked around her, soaking it in. They were standing in the living room – and it was beautiful. The rough-hewn wood glowed in the sunset, the flat grey stones of the fireplace offering a shimmering counterpoint. The cracks between the logs were neatly sealed up with daub. Wind still whistled through the open holes of the windows and doors, but another day would take care of that.

It would be a home. Neat, snug, and warm.

She looked to Elizabeth, then drew her into her arms. "Thank you so much for everything."

Elizabeth stepped back. "I'm just glad to see you smile like that again. It's been a long time. You deserve this."

Naomi moved to her brother, hugging him tightly. He had always been her rock.

Then she moved to David.

Their eyes held, and then Naomi folded herself against him. His arms came up around her, warm, strong, and she knew.

This was meant to be.

# Chapter 7

Naomi was carefully testing the balance of the door on its new hinges when the soft jingle of sleigh-bells came from down the road. She turned with curiosity. The village was fairly remote to begin with, and especially in the winter there was little traffic through. The supply wagon had come two days ago and wasn't due again for another three.

A pair of tall, proud, brown horses came into view, pulling a massive wagon. It wasn't on sleigh-rails – the thick wheels rolled ponderously through the snow. Lucky the snow was there. With the high-stacked, covered weight loaded on the wagon, it's likely that the wheels would have sunk deeply into mud.

The man driving the wagon was tall, wiry, and pure blond. He wore an elegant black wool coat and a matching black hat. A dark scarf was tucked around his neck.

There was more noise, and Naomi stared in surprise. The man wasn't alone. A nearly identical wagon was behind him, this one helmed by a blonde woman. She was just as elegantly dressed in dark colors and her long, blonde hair was braided down her back.

The mounds beneath the wagon's coverings were lumpy and shapeless; Naomi had a sense that they weren't neat boxes of grain or stores. Rather, they had the lopsided, angular look of furniture and other household goods, tied down for the journey.

The horses pulled to a stop before Naomi's new house. William and David came out from their window-work to nod a greeting to the strangers.

The man looked down from his perch. "You, there. Is your master at home?"

Naomi could see the line of tension draw across her brother's shoulders. William's voice was cool when he responded. "I'm my own man. Name's William. William Jackson. This here is my brother-in-law, David Oxendine."

The blond examined both men. "Well then, you can call me Walter Adams." He motioned back over his shoulder. "The lovely lady with me is my devoted wife, Barbara." He raised his eyes to sweep them across the small scattering of buildings before him. "We have been sent down from Nashville to be your new tavern owner and school teacher."

He said it as if he were descending from Heaven on high to mission to the heathens.

William's brow creased. "Tavern owner? I didn't realize old Lowery was finally selling his tavern."

Walter laughed. "No, no, I'm not taking over that old dump. I received ample research about what *that* place is like. No, I'm setting up a new tavern. On the other side of the general store."

Jeff came out to brush down his hands. "What? I thought that land was going to be used for a schoolhouse?"

Walter nodded. "That's right."

Jeff's brow scrunched. "I'm confused. Are you saying those *in the pines* folks at the fool capital sent you out here to set up a second tavern for our town, in the school house?"

Walter's laugh echoed across the village. It was surprising how such a rich belly-laugh could come from such a slender man. "No, no, of course not. Our fine new governor, the honorable Willie Blount, sent us to elevate you to modern standards."

Naomi held in a shiver. She'd heard at Sunday sermons how Governor Blount had been making efforts to send all those with Indian blood to resettle west of the Mississippi. Thank all that was Holy that his idea hadn't gained traction amongst the rest of the government.

*Yet.*

Walter smiled expansively at the group clustered beneath him. "Governor Blount has wisely sent my Barbara here to educate you rustics. Get you speaking proper English."

His eyes shone. "And I'm along to provide entertainment for the adults."

Barbara's voice eased into the mix, a cultured sharpness to her words. "That is right, my dear husband. After all, the children will be in my domain from dawn until just after noon. That is all their small heads can hold. And then that building would just lay vacant until the next day." She tittered. "What an obscene waste!"

She nodded in agreement with her own wisdom. "It's far more efficient to make proper use of the land and heated-up building for the afternoon and evening as well."

William's brow creased. "You'll have men drinking hard liquor at the student's desks?"

Barbara shook her head in mirth. "No, no, of course not. The grown men would hardly fit!" She motioned as if drawing a diagram on a large chalk-board. "The building will be built in two halves, with opposite entrances. Logically, they will share a central heating system. That way when the classes let out, all that heat won't be wasted. It will simply now be going to keep the drinking men warm through the rest of their long, libation-filled evening."

William's lips pursed. Naomi could see he still felt uncomfortable with the idea.

Barbara looked over the house before them. "Just finishing up a building project, I see. Perhaps a bit rustic, but it seems serviceable enough."

She nodded if coming to a decision. "What are your rates?"

William shook his head. "We're building this for my sister, here. Naomi. We're her kin."

Barbara automatically corrected, "Family. You're her family." She nodded again. "I see. So how much would you charge to build a large one-floor structure? It will contain one double-faced fireplace in its center. There shall be sturdy walls to separate out the two halves."

William shook his head. "Mrs. Adams, I don't think you –"

"Two hundred," announced Barbara. "We'll pay you two hundred dollars, to split amongst you, to get it built."

William blinked, then looked to David.

Barbara's voice carried imperious calm. "We need this built as quickly as humanly possible. The government has received a mandate to educate its masses." Her voice grew and swelled, as if speaking to countless numbers of adoring listeners. "A country is based on its literacy, after all. We need stronger, smarter workers. Legions of educated scholars. Especially if we're about to go to war."

Naomi shuddered, drawing back in on herself. She wished by all that was Holy that there would be no more wars. She had heard enough stories of the American Revolution to last a lifetime.

William looked over to where the Carter brothers stood in a quiet huddle. "What were your plans?"

Jim glanced at the others, then took a step forward. "We are your men until you say we are done, William. And then we'll gather our things and head out west, to our uncle's ranch. Once we're there, we're to do whatever he asks until he determines we've paid our debt."

His eyes looked not resigned nor upset, simply calmly accepting of a sequence of events that was proper and right. "So if you want us to help with this, we'll help."

"I'll pay you your due share," commented William. "It might help you pay your way along your journey. It's going to be a long, hard road."

"We don't mind that none. We'll make it somehow. But we appreciate the offer. Could use some better boots and coats before we make a start of it."

He gave a slight smile. "And I a-wanted to get young Hiram a juvember of his own before we left. He's been hankering for one ever since he saw me take down a crow with mine."

Barbara's lips turned down. "A slingshot. Those are slingshots." She rolled her eyes heavenward. "I can see I'll have my work cut out for me in these heathen backwaters."

She drew her gaze in again to pin William. "So, can you start tomorrow?"

William looked back at Naomi's house. "We are pretty much set here. Just have to finish up a few things."

She nodded. "All right, then. We'll expect to see you at dawn, sharp, on the other side of the general store. I heard the owner there is a bit slow, but honest."

Jeff blinked, then stepped forward. "I am Jeff Mason, the owner."

Barbara seemed wholly unconcerned that she had just disparaged the man to his face. "Good to meet you. We'll need all sorts of supplies, of course, as we get settled in. I'll come by tomorrow morning to present you with a list." Her brow narrowed. "You can read, I assume."

He blushed and nodded.

"Good. Well, we're off to Pastor Smith's. We were told that he would put us up for the night."

Pastor Smith winced, running a hand through his hair. "Of course, I would be honored. My house is always open."

"Good," agreed Barbara. "Please lead the way. We've been on the road all day. We are exhausted and hungry."

Elizabeth nudged a head at Naomi. "We'll come along to handle dinner. It's the least we can do, with you being new to town and all."

Barbara gave a shake to her reins. "Good. I hope you have some cinnamon and nutmeg. I do like it so with my yams. And about the chicken I assume we'll be having for our main course – do you feed them …"

Naomi let the words drift in one ear and out the other. She knew Elizabeth would take care of all the details once they got into Pastor Smith's well-kept home. She also knew that Amanda would keep an eye on the four kids until they returned. She was more concerned about this pair of blonde strangers who had descended from On High into their mix.

Was it her imagination, or had Barbara and Walter looked down at the natives of the village as if the locals were rats ravaging a trash heap? Naomi had a sense that, if Barbara had her way, everyone would be speaking in the clipped language and tight formality of whatever she had learned off in Nashville. After all, a juvember was simply a juvember. Naomi had never heard it called anything else, never mind a "sling-shot."

The way her friends and family spoke was a part of the way they were. It was their heritage. So many words were interminglings of Lumbee and African, of Portuguese and simply phrases they'd rolled together over time.

Pastor Smith loved to call his coffee "ellick" – as did several of the other older folk in the area. Was this new schoolteacher going to scold them for that? Tell them their word wasn't the right one?

Her thoughts were shaken free as the two sets of horses wearily drew to a halt before the barn. She lent a hand as the group drew off the harnesses and led the worn-out steeds over to the water trough. The animals seemed quite grateful to be in the warm structure with the other horse and animals. The barn wasn't huge, but it had enough open space at its center to handle the new steeds, at least for now.

Naomi glanced up at Barbara. The blonde was gazing around her in the way an explorer might stare in superior amusement at a group of feral children.

Naomi cleared her throat. "Excuse me, but if William, David, and the others are going to be building your schoolhouse, are you two planning on living there?"

Naomi's laughter was tinkling of icicles. "Oh, no, of course not. Once they're done with the schoolhouse and tavern, we'll have them build us a large home next to it. But the schoolhouse comes first, of course. My salary only begins the day it opens, and we want that to be as soon as possible."

Walter nodded in agreement. "And the tavern, too, of course. Get those thirsty men what they need."

Naomi's brow creased. "We do already have a tavern of our own. Lowery's tavern."

Walter chuckled. "As if any rural tavern owner in this backwards neck of the wood could hold his own against my business degree. I know everything there is to know about how to draw in the drinkers." His mouth drew into a satisfied smirk. "I'd like to see this Lowery fellow stay open for a month, after I get my efforts rolling into high gear."

Naomi pressed her lips together. While there was certainly a share of trouble over at Lowery's, she never had the sense that it was his fault. He tried to provide a warm, calm meeting spot for locals to gather together and share news.

Barbara clapped her hands together. "Well, we won't get fed hanging around in the stables with the horses." She laughed merrily. "Where's the dining room?"

Pastor Smith waved a hand. "Right this way. Let me show you up to the guest room, first, so you can get yourself settled."

Barbara pointed at the wagon. "My trunk is right in there. Right on the back, so it's easy for you to get to it."

Naomi stepped forward. "I'll take care of that. Don't worry."

It didn't seem that Barbara was worried in the least. She turned without a second glance to follow Pastor Smith into the house.

It took Naomi three tries to get the trunk safely down out of the wagon. She wondered how many dead bodies were stuffed into it. It weighed more than Bill had, when she had to lug his drunken body into bed. She slid the trunk along the snow, then into the back door.

Pastor Smith's house was simply but neatly adorned. His kitchen table was polished smooth and had a long bench on either side. His living room had two plump couches. Nearly every member of his congregation had sat on those couches at one point or another in their life, to share their grief or soak in words of wisdom. A gentle fire crackled in the fireplace.

It took Naomi a few minutes to haul the trunk – step by step – up the stairs. She reached the closed door of the guest room and gently knocked.

Barbara drew open the door. "Oh, there you are. Just put it over there, at the foot of the bed."

Naomi nodded and pulled the trunk into place. It was a fine piece of equipment, with sturdy leather straps and a fine brass lock.

Barbara spoke over her shoulder. "We'll be ready in about twenty minutes. Please let the cook know that.

Naomi's mouth twitched in a smile. "I'll let Elizabeth know."

She shook her head as she went back down the stairs. She had a sense, already, that these new members of their little village might fit as well as a pumpkin seed in a mess of crows.

# Chapter 8

It was long past dark when Naomi and Elizabeth headed back toward home. Barbara and William were safely asleep, having exhausted themselves with the long day of travel and then stuffing themselves with a bate of pork, collard greens, and mashed potatoes. For folk who seemed fairly above the rural life, the two newcomers certainly ate like a pair of farmers when the food was put in front of them.

Naomi looked up as they made their way down the snowy street. Elizabeth's house was dim, and she wondered if any candles were lit at all. But in comparison, her new house glowed with life. A lit candle flickered in every window. A stream of smoke drifted up from the new fireplace. And a freshly-made wreath of pine needles hung on her front door.

She drew to a stop, tears welling in her eyes.

Elizabeth came up alongside her, smiling. She waited a long moment, allowing Naomi time to absorb the vision before her.

Then she gently took Naomi by the arm. "Come on. Let's head into your new home."

A chorus of cheers welcomed them as they pushed open the front door. Naomi blinked in surprise. The old table from the shack was there, but William had done an amazing job of shoring it into fresh life. It boasted a fresh coat of varnish and shone with a golden glow. The chairs around it had new cushions of burgundy cloth.

A fire crackled in the fireplace, and a pair of ivory pillar candles sat on the mantle. On the wall opposite hung the drawing of the Irish village made by her father.

Naomi's eyes filled freshly with tears, and she shook her head at William. "I can't take that! That hung in your bedroom!"

William came over to give her a fond hug. "I've had it for fifteen years now, Naomi. Ever since our father passed away. It's time for you to take your turn. And you have the space to hang it in your main living room, where everybody can enjoy it. It's just right."

Johnny jumped up and down at her feet. He cried out, "Our beds are upstairs! In our new room! We have a room of our own!"

William nodded. "And we got your bed up into your room, Naomi. It's a bit lumpy, but I cobbled it together as best we can. It'll have to do for now, until I can get around to –"

She drew him again into a hard hug, crying now. "You are too good for me. Thank you. Thank you for everything."

Amanda called from the dining area. "We figured you guys ate with the Pastor, so we fed the kids already. But I did make some chess pie, and some strong apple cider. A celebration, for your first real day in your new home."

Naomi's mouth watered, and she moved into the kitchen.

*Her kitchen.*

The thought still amazed her. It was beautiful. A large window looked out over the back yard. She could see the moon rising over the trees, sending its silvery glow across the snow. It was like something out of a fairy tale.

Amanda handed around gorgeous pottery mugs done in swirls of tan and brown, and Naomi held hers for a long while, soaking in the warmth of it – the warmth of everything.

Elizabeth raised her mug up. "A toast! To Naomi, and her new beginning."

"To Naomi!"

The mugs clinked, and Naomi drew them in. For so many years she had been a part of this village and at the same time in complete isolation. Bill had seen sure of that. But finally – at long last – she was free. And already her life had changed in ways she could never have imagined.

She looked down at her two young children, at the wreaths of smiles on their faces. And she knew that everything had been worth it. Every hardship, every hurdle, every hiccup along the way, for they had all brought her here.

To safety.

The chess pie was eaten, the cider was drunk, and farewells were made to her guests. She closed her door as William left, slid the sturdy bolt in place, and then she looked around. Fresh burgundy curtains hung at each window, pulled shut against the night. The fire crackled low in the fireplace, its gentle warmth easing across the room. There was a magical glow across everything. It shimmered across the drawing on the wall, of her father's distant Irish home. It glowed against the colorful mugs which were now a part of her world.

It shone down on her two beautiful children.

She drew Polly up in her arms, and then took Johnny by the hand. "Come on, Let's get you two up to bed."

She crested the top of the stairs and then looked to the right, to where the children's room was. Then she looked down at them both. "How about, for this first night, we all sleep together in the same room? It's a new place, and it might make noises as it settles in. Log cabins are like that. I wouldn't want you worried about a jubous noise in the night."

Johnny nodded with shining eyes. "A-course, Mama. I'll protect you."

Naomi's eyes glistened, and she drew her young son close. "I know you would, my little sow cat."

She drew them into her bedroom. Her bed had a new, burgundy kiver on it, quilted and warm, and the matching curtains were drawn. Elizabeth's dream-catcher hung over the bed.

Naomi's eyes threatened to overrun. It was all just so much to take in. Her family had gone above and beyond in their quest to make her feel at ease in her new home.

She drew back the kiver and climbed into bed, laying Polly next to her. Johnny climbed in on the other side, and the blanket felt like pure heaven as she drew it up over them. The little tin candle holder was on her dresser, sending its soft light across the room, but now her bedroom was no longer a place of despair and sadness. Now it brought her joy and contentment.

Johnny murmured sleepily at her side. "Mama, tell us a story."

Naomi's heart warmed. In the past he would have been nervous about asking – fearing the wrath of their drunken father. Now he asked simply as a joy for them to share. A way for them to connect at the end of a long, wonderful day.

"Of course, sweetheart. What would you like to hear?"

He nuzzled against her. "Tell us one of grandpa's stories. His ones from Ireland."

She pressed a kiss against his forehead. "All right, my darling. I wish he was still alive, to tell you them himself. He had this great, rich voice and the stories came alive in his Irish brogue. But I'll do the best I can."

She looked down. "How about I tell you the story of Queen Medb?"

Johnny nodded. "Queen May-eve," he repeated, stretching out the name.

"That's her. She was an amazing, inspirational woman. Wise. Intelligent. Strong. A great warrior. She was beautiful, too. She was respected by everyone she met. Back in the olden days of Ireland, relationships were often temporary. A man and a woman would get together for a while, spend time, and if things didn't work out, they would part ways again."

Johnny murmured, "Like you and Dada."

Naomi's heart breathed in. She was grateful that Johnny was taking the change so smoothly. She had been worried that he'd miss his father or long for him to return. But it seemed, instead, that

Johnny seemed to take his departure as a natural, even good thing.

Now she just had to make sure she did a better job of raising her son alone than the Carter mother had.

She brushed back Johnny's hair. "Yes, like me and your papa," she agreed. "We spent some time together, and it was not healthy for us. So we each went our separate ways."

Johnny nodded, accepting this without comment.

Naomi looked at the small faces alongside her. "In the same way, Queen Medb spent time with various partners, to determine who was best suited to be with her. One of these men was Conchobar mac Nessa, a strong warrior in his own right. Unfortunately, Queen Medb felt that she was being used to seal a treaty and not respected for who she was as a person. So she left Conchobar to seek out a man who respected her."

Johnny nodded. "Someone who loved her."

"Exactly my sweet. So instead she tried being with the King of Connact, Tinni mac Conri. But this didn't work out either. Neither man was just what she wanted."

"So what did she do?"

"Well, my darling, her life was quite dangerous, and through it all her bodyguard stayed loyally at her side. Ailill was always there for her. No matter what. He proved himself over and over again. And finally her eyes opened and she realized he was the one for her."

Johnny's eyes opened. "She left a King to be with a soldier?"

"She did indeed. Because she knew in the end what she needed was not wealth or power – but someone who cared for her deeply. Someone who was loyal to her. Someone who would protect her."

Johnny smiled. "Oh! Someone like Uncle David."

A glow soared through Naomi, and she looked down at her small son. It took her a moment to put breath behind her words. "Sweetie, what do you think of David?"

He closed his eyes again, nuzzling against her. "I like Uncle David. He makes me feel safe. When he puts me up on his shoulders, I feel like I could do anything. Anything at all."

Naomi closed her eyes, drawing her two children in against her warmth.

"I know exactly what you mean."

# Chapter 9

Dawn shimmered its golden fingers across her kitchen table, and her cup of coffee sat steaming before her. Johnny and Polly were playing on the floor in front of the fireplace, stacking small wooden blocks on top of each other. There were piles and piles of those blocks, left over from the house construction, and Naomi intended to spend some time carving shapes into them for her children. William might have the keen woodcarving skills, but she could do her best to make a fish or cat with her own pocket knife.

There was a knock on her door.

Deep fear dug into Naomi. Bill had come back for her. He had come back for them all.

She drew in deep, long breaths. She forced herself to focus. Bill was gone. He was long gone, off across the Mississippi, and her new life had begun.

She recited the mantra as a blanket to protect her.

She wrapped her robe closely around her flannel nightgown, then moved to the door. She undid the latch and cracked it open a notch. "Who is it?"

David stood there, smiling at her.

Deep relief coursed through her. She drew the door wide. "Welcome! I thought you and William were going over to work on the school house today."

He chuckled. "You mean the tavern, don't you? Yes, I'm sure the Carter brothers are over there already, ready to get to work."

His brow shadowed. "I know I should hate those men for what they nearly did to you. And yet, against all odds, I do think there is good in their souls. Somehow life twisted them, somewhere along the way. But even in just these past days I've watched them substantially change."

His eyes softened. "The way they act with the children … it's heart-warming. I think they'd been hardened by life. Calloused against a nasty world. And their mother built those callouses on them. But it's like they've finally found a spring, after a long, hard winter. They're gentling."

Naomi gave a smile. "That's good to hear. I like to hope that every person has the opportunity to better themselves."

David's eyes twinkled. "Even Barbara and Walter?"

Naomi chuckled. "Especially those two. They've probably spent their entire life in the state capital surrounded by wealth and high-speaking politicians. They don't even know what it is to do work for themselves." Her eyes shone. "They'll be in for a rude awakening the first night they're left alone in that new house of theirs and have to figure out how to take care of themselves."

"Maybe not. I hear tell they're looking to hire a house-maid. Someone to keep the place clean, do their cooking, that sort of thing."

Naomi blinked. "That sounds like something I could do."

He tilted his head. "But you have the two children. What would happen to them?"

"I could ask Elizabeth to keep an eye on them. She's home with Hiram anyway. And I could share out my money with her in thanks."

"Is that what you want?"

She looked around her new home. "I don't know what I want. It's all been so sudden. I can barely take it all in. But I know I have received so many blessings in life that I want to pay them back, somehow. And right now I have nothing. Nothing but what you all have given me. So I have to find my way to earn a path."

His brow creased. "Well, don't take any action too quickly. Give yourself some time to settle in and think about things. Figure out what you want to do."

"You're right, of course. I'll try to do that. It's just all so new to me. I haven't had the ability to think about my own goals and dreams in ... well, in forever, it seems."

He smiled at her. "Even more reason to take it slow and to savor this. Take your time. It's winter. Spring is a long time off."

Johnny came galloping over, a dowel of wood in his hand. "Aillil! Aillil! Are you here for Queen Medb?"

Naomi blushed – she could feel her cheeks flaming with heat. "I'm sorry, I was just telling him –"

David gave a laugh. "The story of Queen Medb and her lovers, apparently."

Naomi's flush coursed down her entire body.

David dropped to one knee before Johnny. "So you don't think I'm Conchobar mac Nessa?"

Johnny emphatically shook his head. "Conchobar wasn't good enough. She left him. She wanted someone who would love her. Who would protect her and respect her."

David's voice became low and rough with emotion. "And you think I am that man?"

Johnny nodded. "Of course! Aren't you?"

David reached a hand out to tenderly stroke Johnny's cheek. He didn't speak.

After a moment he stood, nodding to Naomi. "Elizabeth's going to make a ham tonight, to celebrate Twelfth Night."

Johnny looked up. "What's Twelfth Night?"

"It's when the wise men arrived at the manger, to discover the baby Jesus in his crib. We celebrate the recognition of his Holiness by the wise and learned of the world."

David looked over to Elizabeth. "Will you come by and join us? Or did you want to spend some time alone in your new home?"

She smiled at him. "I would gladly join you. After all, these holidays only come once a year. I'll have plenty of time to enjoy my house once these holidays are behind us."

His gaze shadowed, and he nodded. "I'll see you tonight, then." He gave a fond tousle to Johnny's head, and then he was out the door.

Elizabeth closed the door with a nagging concern in her heart. The holidays were coming to an end. David had only come up from his father's home in South Carolina to spend the holidays with his sister. He could hardly sleep on her living room floor for months on end.

But if he left …

Johnny looked up at her. "Mama? Are you all right?"

She nodded down at him. "I'm right as rain, sweetheart. Don't you worry about me. Now let's see what we can do with these blocks of yours."

\* \* \*

Naomi cradled her bowl of mashed potatoes in her arm as she knocked on the door. It was all she could make with the supplies salvaged from her old home, but it would have to do. She wanted to bring something to the dinner tonight.

Elizabeth pulled open the door and smiled at her. "Let's start with a new rule. Our houses are open to each other, all day, all night, any time. You and your family can just walk in any time you want and we'll do the same. Our kids can run back and forth as if we're one big family, which we are. What do you think about that?

Johnny smiled. "Yes!"

Hiram peered over from the fire. "Look at these blocks I have from your house! They're house blocks!"

Johnny grinned. "I have some too! Let's see!" He ran over to take a look. "Wow, Uncle William made some cool shapes in yours. That one looks like a pumpkin seed!"

"And that one's Pastor Smith's Horse," agreed Hiram. "Let's figure them all out!"

Naomi smiled at William as she took off her coat and boots. "You are so good to the boys."

"I enjoy it," he replied. "Gives me something to do in the evenings, and it's simple enough. Hiram gets such pleasure out of it. I'll make some for Johnny, too."

"I'm going to give it a try, as well. See what I can make."

"Good for you! It's a good craft to learn now. That way it'll keep you occupied when you're old and feeble."

She nudged him in the ribs. "That's why we're side by side. So we can take care of each other in our dotage."

She glanced at David in the kitchen, and she dropped her eyes. David's father was in his dotage – and he relied on his son to take care of him. But the father was down in South Carolina, and David was up here, on his last days. When that tavern was finished – or maybe when the house that was to be built after it – his time here would be complete. And then he'd be gone … gone …

Elizabeth took the bowl of mashed potatoes from her. "These look lovely, Naomi. Thank you so much for bringing them. I'm sure they'll make a wonderful addition to our meal."

Naomi breathed in the rich scents that flowed over the room. There was a hint of cinnamon in the aroma, and a thought came to her. "What of the newcomers – and Pastor Smith? Have you left him to fend for himself?"

Elizabeth smiled, shaking his head. "Amanda went over there with Jessica. The village women are taking turns lending a hand. They all want to get a sense of the couple, too, so the volunteers are gladly signing up. They want to see just what kind of a woman will be instructing their children."

William's mouth turned down. "Instructing is right," he murmured. "She wants to stamp out all sign of who we are and turn us into cookie-cutters of the capital politicians."

Naomi smiled at her brother. "She's new to the region, still. Let's give her some time. Maybe that shiny newness of her quest will wear off and she'll become more human."

He looked doubtful. "We'll see." His eyes brightened. "But in the meantime, let's eat! My mouth is rumbling loud enough to wake a hibernating frog."

Hiram giggled loudly. "You can't wake 'em, Papa! They're asleep!"

William tousled Hiram's head. "That they are, my little sow cat. Now come on over to the table."

The table was filled, hands were clasped, and grace was said. Naomi smiled as the food was passed around. It was almost seeming normal.

Being surrounded by friends and family. Good food. Warmth. Love, Comfort.

There was a nagging sense that this was all temporary – that something would happen to rip it away from her, but she put it off. She would cling to this as tightly as she could.

These was a noise from outside. A low thumping.

She froze.

David looked up and his brow creased in concern. "What is it, Naomi?"

She looked at the door. "I heard something."

He stood and went over to the window, drawing aside the curtain to peer out. He chuckled. "Just a hungry deer coming to nibble at one of the saplings. It'll move on once it gets those last few leaves."

Naomi willed her shoulders to ease. Bill was gone. Nobody had seen hide nor hair of him since that night he'd run off. And, besides, she had a house full of loyal friends to help keep her safe.

At last the meal was finished and William nodded to Hiram. "All right, Hiram, it's time for you to fetch the wreath."

Johnny looked up. "Why is he getting the wreath, Mama?"

She smiled down at him. "It's twelfth night, Johnny. The wreaths come down tonight, and all the nuts and berries that decorated them get eaten.

It's all to celebrate the discovery of the Baby Jesus."

Hiram ran to the front door, drawing it open.

Naomi's heart leapt at the dark shadows beyond. She could swear Bill was out there, just waiting for his chance.

To her surprise, the street beyond was empty. Just moonlight streaming down on glistening snow.

Elizabeth leant over. "Are you sure you're all right, Naomi?"

She drew a smile on her face. "I'm fine, really. Just my stomach getting used to this rich food."

Elizabeth smiled. "Well, you'd better get used to it soon, because this is just the way it's going to be for now on."

Hiram drew down the wreath and pushed closed the door. Then he brought the wreath over to lay at the center of the table.

There were a wealth of delights on it. Pine nuts, blackberries, raspberries, and other treats, mostly dried, but all wonderful. Each person took their turn, selecting something, and by the time the wreath was empty of its treasures every face glowed with satisfaction.

Hiram's eyes turned to Elizabeth. "Can we hear a story, Mama?"

She smiled. "Shall we all sit in front of the fire?"

Hiram and Johnny nodded enthusiastically and ran over to clear their bocks out of the way. In a few minutes the adults had moved over to join them, taking their seats and relaxing against chairs, pillows, or the wall.

Elizabeth smiled at the gathered group, nestled against her husband. William's arm was resting gently around his wife. Naomi felt a twinge echo through her heart. *This* is what she wanted. Even with so much she already had, this hollow still existed – this desire for that loving connection in her own world. A tender father for Johnny and Polly. A support for herself.

She looked down at her hands.

*If only David would stay.*

Elizabeth's voice eased into her thoughts, gentle and warm. "Why don't I tell you one of the stories of Anansi the spider?"

Hiram clapped his hands in delight.

Johnny looked up. "Who is Anansi?"

Elizabeth nodded. "Anansi was a god of our ancestors in Africa. Along the beautiful coastline where the ocean meets the land and the sun is warm.

Her voice took on the rich tenor of a storyteller. "Anansi was a small spider, to be sure. And perhaps not very strong. But Anansi was smart, which was most important of all. Anansi might not be able to overpower his oppressors, or take direct action against them, but through perseverance and careful action he could achieve his goals."

Johnny leant against his elbows, spellbound.

Elizabeth looked across the room, lit in its flickering firelight and tapered candles. "Now note, my children, that I do not necessarily say that this story I'm about to share is true. It is a story. No more, no less. Listen to the story, and think about it. The function of a story is to help you think. And that is what Anansi is all about."

The room waited in hushed silence.

"Many, many years ago, when the sun and the moon were still children in the night sky, and our cities and towns were but a dream within a dream, there was Anansi. Anansi longed for stories, but all the stories were hoarded by Nyame, the God of the sky. So Anansi went to Nyame to ask if he could have some, to share with the world.

"The sky god was a very jealous god, and he did not want to share his stories. So he set Anansi on impossible tasks. He told Anansi to try to capture Onini, the great python. Nyame knew there was no chance that a tiny, delicate spider could take down a massive python.

"Anansi thought and thought about how he could capture such a powerful beast. He studied the python and found that the python was very boastful. The snake's weakness was his pride. So

Anansi walked along in the python's presence and commented about how the python seemed short. Surely the python was not as long as a palm branch.

"The python was outraged, knowing full well that he was as long as that branch, if not longer! So he insisted that he prove his massive and impressive size.

"When the python tried to stretch himself straight, his body kept trying to curl back up again. So Anansi offered to help by tying the python to the branch, to help him measure to his full glorious height.

"The python gladly agreed."

Hiram giggled in delight, and his mother smiled fondly at him.

"Once Anansi had the python fully and securely tied to the branch, he brought the captive back to the sky god, and proclaimed his victory.

"The sky god was frustrated. How did this little spider achieve such a task? He set Anansi out on another task, even harder than the first. He insisted Anansi had to capture Osebo the leopard. Surely there was no way that a tiny little spider could take on a massive leopard, with its razor teeth and needle-sharp claws.

"Again, Anansi was careful in his approach. He used attentive observation to learn what he could about Osebo. He quickly found that Osebo loved to bound and leap around the forest. So Anansi determinedly dug a pit on a path that the leopard took each morning to reach the river.

"Sure enough, the leopard ended up falling right into the pit.

"Anansi ran over to help the leopard and said that he'd build a ladder out of web to help the leopard climb out. Once the leopard made it up the pit wall, covered in sticky spider web, it was easy enough for Anansi to finish the job and completely immobilize the leopard. He then brought the sticky captive back to the sky god."

Now Johnny was grinning, enraptured by the story.

"Of course, the sky god was now beyond furious. Two of his traps had failed! He had to think of something even more diabolical. He told little Anansi that he had to gather up the Mmoboro hornets. Surely that would be impossible for a little spider.

"Anansi was not dissuaded. He knew that he could do anything he set his mind to. He might be tiny, and have delicate limbs, but his mind and his perseverance were his greatest skills.

"Anansi realized that in order to catch the hornets he'd have to get them to want to go inside a container. He found an empty gourd which was naturally shaped like a bottle. Now, how to get the hornets to want to go inside it?

"He looked up at the clouds in the sky, and inspiration struck him.

"He took another gourd and filled it with water. He sprinkled some over the hornets' nest and called out to them that it was raining. He warned them that their nest, while sturdy in the sun, might dissolve after a hard rain. He offered to them that they hide out in his bottle gourd during the downpour – and that when it was over they could come out and build a fresh nest.

"The hornets were thrilled at Anansi's kind offer and flew into the safety of the bottle gourd.

"Anansi promptly stoppered it up, and now he had a gourd full of buzzing hornets to present to the sky god."

Polly giggled, her eyes shining in the firelight.

"By this time the sky god was beside himself with anger. How could Anansi keep doing these impossible tasks? So he decided to find one last task which was beyond all others. This involved a magical man – Mmoatia, a dwarf.

"The dwarfs in this part of the world were feisty and quick-tempered. Anansi thought and thought of a way to make this part of his plan. Finally he had it.

"He made a delicious bowl of yams. And then he found a life-like doll and covered it with sticky tar. He put the bowl and the doll in a place that the dwarves liked to walk.

"Sure enough, a dwarf came along, saw the yams, and asked if the child minded if he had some. When the child did not respond, he ate a yam and loved it. He then thanked the child. But the child, of course, did not reply.

"This made the dwarf upset – he thought the child was ignoring him. So he pushed hard at the child to get him to pay attention. His hand got stuck in the glue. When he tried to pry himself free, his other hand, and soon his whole body was stuck against that doll.

"When Anansi returned to the sky god with this latest capture, the sky god knew that he had met with defeat. Anansi was truly up to any task set for him. The sky god gave Anansi the stories, and Anansi then shared them with the entire world."

Elizabeth smiled at the group. "This is our story for the evening. If you like it, please share it with others. For this is how our stories grow and help all."

Johnny, Hiram, and Polly all clapped their hands with enthusiasm. Johnny glowed. "That was a great story!"

Elizabeth blushed. "Thank you very much, little sow cat. Now I would have to bet it's your bedtime."

Johnny's mouth opened in a wide yawn, and Naomi smiled. "Luckily, we're right next door, so it's not far at all to go."

Elizabeth nodded. "I am so glad you're there, Naomi."

Naomi gathered up her children and tucked them into their coats and boots. "Shall we see you tomorrow for Sunday's service?"

Elizabeth nodded. "And then for the feast of the Epiphany, afterwards. I have the twelfth-cake all ready to go. We'll see who our King and Queen for the day are!"

Johnny grinned. "My Mama is the Queen! Queen Maeve! And that makes David the King!"

William and Elizabeth turned amused eyes to the couple.

Naomi blushed furiously. "It's time for us to go, little one. C'mon."

She didn't dare look up as she bundled her two little children out into the snow – and into the home of their own.

She carried them up the stairs and into their very own room. She laid Polly into her crib, nestled in a new, dark-brown blanket of soft wool. Then Johnny climbed in on his mat with its own fresh kiver over the top. He looked up at her with big eyes. "Are you sure you'll be all right on your own tonight, Mama? If you get scared, you can always come and get me."

She smiled down at him. "You are very sweet, little one. And the same goes for you, you know. I'm right there across the hall."

He shook his head. "We are safe here," he promised. "Nothing can get to us. Because Uncle David and Uncle William built it."

She pressed a kiss on him. "You are absolutely right. Now sleep well, because tomorrow is a big day."

# Chapter 10

Naomi's heart pounded against her chest as her family walked down the snowy lane toward the beautiful church. It was picture-perfect. Snow drifted in soft waves along the sides of the road. The horses murmured to each other in the barn behind the Pastor's house. A small rabbit hopped along the road, leaving delicate footprints in its wake. Ahead of her she could see Jeff and Amanda come out of the general store, Jessica swinging on their hands between them. Pastor Smith was at his place at the steps, greeting everyone. She imagined that Barbara and Walter were already inside, taking the very best pews for themselves.

She peered in the open doors as they approached. Sure enough, there the two newcomers were. Dressed as if for a presidential inauguration and gazing around them in cautious curiosity, as if they expected headhunters to leap out from behind the shadows.

Pastor smith drew her into a warm hug as she reached him. His voice was rich with compassion. "My child, your new home is beautiful. Happy Epiphany. We have reached the end – and the beginning. It is the end of the holiday season. It is the beginning of a fresh new year – one where we celebrate the life and sacrifices of our lord Jesus Christ."

A shadow of dread slunk through Naomi's soul, and she forced herself to smile and nod. It seemed that every turn was reminding her that the holidays were over. Twelfth night was over. Epiphany would soon be over. And that would be it. There would be nothing left to hold David with them. Nothing left to hold his amber eyes and rich voice to stay with their family.

The faint glimmer of a thought came to her. She could go down to south Carolina with him, could relocate the two young children.

She shook her head. As much as David warmed her soul, she knew she just could not do it. Not with the beautiful new house freshly built for her. Not with David and Elizabeth having poured themselves into making this new start for her. She could not uproot all of that to take a wild chance, no matter how honorable David seemed. She had learned that lesson. She would stand on her own two feet and be in a place that brought her joy and stability. Then she would find a man who fit into that life as if it was meant to be.

Johnny raced ahead to be with Hiram, and Elizabeth took Polly from Naomi's arms, bouncing her gently as she and William moved down the aisle. Naomi saw that Jeff and his family took the pew behind them. Young Jessica, wearing a lovely, freshly-pressed dress in dark blue, leaned forward over the pew to whisper something in Hiram's ear. He blushed bright red and nodded.

A warm voice came from over Naomi's shoulder. "Naomi?"

She turned, her cheeks warming. David was there, looking down at her.

Her gaze moved up his body, reached his face, and a chill twined in her heart. His brow was creased and shadowed. His throat seemed tight as he said, "Naomi, I … I need to talk with you."

Dread drifted even stronger into Naomi's chest, nearly smothering her. This was it. He needed to warn her that he was leaving soon. That he had enjoyed their time together, but he had other obligations. Of course he did. She had known it all along, that he would have to leave. Leave, leave, and go far away.

*Just like Bill.*

She flushed, looking down at her hands. She shouldn't do that. He was nothing like Bill. David was strong, brave, and loyal. He had stood by her when few others did. He deserved the utmost of respect. He was leaving to care for his family, just as she was doing for her own.

If only things were different …

There was a stir in the church, and she looked back toward the entry doors. The Carter brothers stood there nervously, their faces freshly shaven, their clothes as neat as she'd ever seen them. They looked like foxes caught in a lion's den.

A soft smile came to Naomi's lips. What a change from the previous week. One week ago their presence had been enough to shoot fear through her core. Now she found she had compassion in her heart for the four men.

Time could change so much.

The men carefully set into motion, as if walking on glass, and Jim nodded a welcome as they approached. "Mama made us swear to attend church regular now," he murmured. "And no more drinking all night at a tavern. Just the normal beer with a meal, and that's it."

Pastor Smith smiled warmly at them as he came up behind them. "It's good to see you, boys, whatever the reason. You are always welcome in any house of God."

They seemed uncertain of this, but they slid into a pew opposite Naomi's family. She could almost see an ease to their shoulders as they settled into place. They were like a row of four crows hunkering down on a branch, waiting patiently for the day to pass.

Crows.

Naomi's eyes widened as the word which had once been shouted at her in anger now only brought to mind the intelligent bird. It had been one week. One week and she had not once heard someone call her a crow, or a squaw, or all the other soul-draining phrases that had become so much of her life. She hadn't even realized it until she thought about it. And even more important, her children were now in a place free from all of that hostility.

The thought filled her with a rich glow.

David watched her, his amber eyes far away. His voice was hoarse when he spoke. "We can talk later. I think Pastor Smith is nearly ready to begin."

She nodded, and he slid into place at her side.

Tears welled in her eyes. This was the way things should be. It was the way they should always be. If only she could bottle this moment in time and keep it forever, safe and sound.

But she knew it couldn't be true. Life was always changing and shifting. Alteration was the very nature of life. Her children would grow and mature. Perhaps William and Elizabeth would have another child. Maybe Hiram and Jessica would become fond of each other – or maybe they wouldn't.

The only constant was change. It was her job to trust in God and to be accepting of what happened.

A whisper reminded her that God expected her to take care of herself, too. She had to step up and do what had to be done to keep her family safe. Whatever it took.

Even if it meant turning her back on her own heart.

David's warmth seemed to radiate at her side; she held off the wave of sadness which echoed with it.

*She had to trust.*

Pastor Smith's sermon was full of love and joy, of celebration and contentment. He reminded his flock that the Epiphany was a day of rejoicing. The baby Jesus had been accepted by the wise kings, and His service to mankind was just beginning. He was embarking, first, on a childhood full of gentle love and laughter – a childhood with a loving mother and a tender wood-working father. This formed the foundation which allowed him to weather so many storms, later in life.

Naomi looked over at Elizabeth. In many ways, Elizabeth and her brother reminded her of Mary and Joseph. They loved each other dearly.

They tended to their only son with joyous hearts. William was a fine craftsman. He was known throughout the region for imbuing each wood carving with love and attention. As a result, he earned enough to keep his family well cared for.

Naomi looked at her two young children. If only she could carve out that same peace for her own youngsters.

Her resolve distilled. She would do it. She would find a way – no matter what it took. Like Anansi the spider, she would evaluate her options, think about what her next step should be, and then tackle it with every ounce of energy in her power.

# Chapter 11

Naomi's feet dragged as the family walked the short distance back to Elizabeth's home. The cheery glow of the fire, the bright sparkle of the candles in the window - all of it reminded her of a joy which was about to be extinguished. She unbundled her children and released them to play merrily with blocks before the fire, but her own thoughts were lost in a murky darkness.

There was talking around her, they moved to the table, and the Twelfth Night bread was served. When David found the bean in his slice, Naomi poked at her own, sure that Elizabeth had had a hand in the distribution. Sure enough, there was the pea in her piece. They were the King and Queen of the evening. She was Queen Mabh and he was her King. But she knew the smile on her lips was only skin deep. Her heart sagged with desolation.

Elizabeth looked to William with worry, and his gaze went to David. William nodded at his brother-in-law.

David looked down, drew in a breath, and then stood. "Naomi, would you come talk with me for a few minutes?"

Her heart thundered against her ribs. It took all her control to nod and stand.

He went out with her to the front door. They put on their boots and coats.

They stepped through.

The world was sparkly and new. It really did seem as if the baby Jesus had come into the world to bring it hope and joy. The moonlight glistened off the ice on the trees, making them magical and light. Her own home shone with newness, and her heart soared to take it in.

David walked alongside her to the house, and they went in to her living room. The fire was banked low, giving a cozy, gentle feel to the room. She could barely make out her father's drawing on the opposite wall, of the quiet village he had been taken away from as a child. She knew he had missed it dearly and had always wished he could return. But to travel there just to visit would have been enormously expensive and quite dangerous. So, instead he simply remained in his new home, raising the family he had created.

David's voice came from behind her, hoarse and low. "Naomi … are you happy here?"

She wrapped her arms around her, tensing. She drew in a deep breath before responding. "If you had asked me that a month ago, I would have given a quite different answer. But, yes, I am very happy here. Bill has left to the far ends of the Earth. I am living next to my brother and his family – I love them all dearly. I have the most amazing house I could ever imagine. It is everything I could ask for in life."

She swallowed. "Well, almost everything."

She turned to David. She could see the turmoil of emotion in his eyes; the tension in his shoulders.

His voice was hoarse. "My father … he needs someone to care for him."

Here it was.

She pressed her lips together, willing herself not to cry. She managed to get out the words.

"I know, David. I know."

He took in another deep breath, holding her gaze.

"Naomi, I need to ask you a question."

She blinked. What could he possibly need to ask her? It was already clear. She was the fish in a pond, and he was a bird in the sky. They might care for each other, but their lives were wholly separate. They had responsibilities that drew them in different directions. It simply could not be.

Still, her voice was tight when she spoke.

"What is the question?"

He took a step toward her, gazing down at her.

The front door flew inward off its hinges as if it had been kicked by a bull moose. Snow and darkness swirled into the room, causing the fire to gutter and flicker wildly.

Bill stormed into the room, his eyes burning like the depths of Hades itself, his fists clenched and raw.

"What the Hell is going on here?"

Thank you for reading *In the Pines.* The sequel will be out shortly.

If you enjoyed this novel, please leave feedback on Amazon, Goodreads, and any other systems. Together we can help make a difference!

Be sure to sign up for my free newsletter! You'll get alerts of free books, discounts, and new releases. I run my own newsletter server – nobody else will ever see your email address. I promise! http://www.lisashea.com/lisabase/subscribe.html

Please visit the following pages for news about free books, discounted releases, and new launches. Feel free to post questions there – I strive to answer within a day! Facebook: https://www.facebook.com/LisaSheaAuthor

Twitter: https://twitter.com/LisaSheaAuthor

Google+: https://plus.google.com/+LisaSheaAuthor/posts

Blog: http://www.lisashea.com/lisabase/blog/

Share the news – we all want to enjoy interesting novels!

# About the Story

I have wanted to write this story for a long, long time. Naomi Oxendine, born 1784, is a direct ancestor of mine. She endured a staggering amount of hardship in her life. I am extremely fortunate to have reams of records on her, because of a court case that her son, Johnny, was involved in. Much of the court case centers around race, perceptions of race, and interpretations of race. It is powerful, fascinating, depressing, and instructive, all at once.

Despite those records, there are still great swaths of information which has been lost over the years. Many records were destroyed during the Civil War. I take liberties with those "holes" to create a compelling story – but I strive to stay true to the known facts. My intention is to authentically present the many traumas that Naomi had to endure. To show my enduring respect for her tenacity and spirit in the face of great challenge.

The late 1700s and early 1800s were a tumultuous time in the American South. Irish slavery was just as horrific as African slavery, and yet it's rarely talked about. During those early years, there was often a sense of "we're all in this together" as colonists struggled to survive in a wild, new country. Blacks, whites, Portuguese, Lumbees, and others worked, fought, played, and loved. It was only as life began to become more "civilized" – and there was more to lose – that the whites in power took greater and greater steps to solidify the strata between them and the "others."

The topic of slavery, inter-race relations, and why people do what they do to other people is one that entire college degrees are based around. It would be impossible for me to encompass all the myriad of reasons and factors in short novellas. Still, I think the more we can be aware of what our ancestors went through, and where we came from, the better we can try to understand where we are now and make a path to a better future. For us, and for our next generation.

I am wholeheartedly proud to have Irish blood, Lumbee blood, African blood, and the many other streams which joined together to make me unique. I would hope that, someday, we can respect all people, of all colors, shapes, sizes, and backgrounds, and treasure them for their unique beauty and style.

In the end, we are all kin.

# Naomi Oxendine

Naomi Oxendine, the historical one, was born in 1784 in Guilford County, North Carolina. She was the fifth of five children born to William Jackson. William had had the first with one wife, and then the remaining four with Margareth Liviston.

In the 1790 census Naomi was living with that family. Her father was still alive. He passed away in 1792.

Naomi's brother, William, married Elizabeth Oxendine sometime before 1800. There's no census for 1800 or 1810 because of the wars.

We know that in 1807 that Johnny was born, the child of Naomi and Bill Williams. In 1809 they had Polly. There's no record of Bill marrying Naomi.

That takes us as far as this second story ☺.

# Glossary of Terms

Living in the 1800s in rural Tennessee meant absorbing a wealth of languages. There were Africans and Portuguese. Lumbee Indians and Irish. The flavors intermingled, and many of the words and terms can still be heard today.

A-gonna / a-fixin' / a-hopin': It was and is common in this area to add an "a" before –ing style verbs.

Chunked: tossed, threw

Fixin' To: planning to

Gyp - female dog. A kinder term than the B one.

Haint – ghost. Now often pronounced as 'haunt'

In the pines - wealthy

Meddlin' – interfering. Many of us now associate it with Scooby Doo and the "meddlin' kids" ☺

Pappy sack – playful nickname for a child

Pumpkin seed – a type of sunfish. Pumpkin seeds are easily-caught fish found all along the East Coast.

You See Me - do you understand?

# **Dedication**

To the Boston Writer's Group, which supports me in all my writing quests.

To Ruth, who provides valuable insight into my efforts.

To Bobbie and Steve from my Oxendine research group for their wonderful support.

To my dad, George Waller, and to his mother, Jane Waller. Both of them adore genealogy and did immense amounts of research into the Oxendine family line. I owe much of my knowledge of this part of history to their efforts.

# About the Author

All proceeds from the *Oxendine* series benefits local battered women's shelters.

Lisa has written 41 fiction books, 81 non-fiction books, and 36 short stories.

**Lisa's medieval romance novels:**
Seeking the Truth
Knowing Yourself
A Sense of Duty
Creating Memories
Looking Back
Badge of Honor
Lady in Red
Finding Peace
Believing your Eyes
Trusting in Faith
Sworn Loyalty
In A Glance

Each novel is a stand-alone story set in medieval England. The novels can be read in any order and have entirely separate casts of characters.

**Lisa's modern murder mystery series:**
Aspen Allegations
Birch Blackguards
Cedar Conundrums

**Lisa's sci-fi romance series:**
Aquarian Awakenings
Betelgeuse Beguiling
Centauri Chaos
Draconis Discord

**Lisa's dystopian series:**
Into the Wasteland
He Who Was Living
Broken Images

**Lisa's regency time-travel series:**
One Scottish Lass
A Time Apart
A Circle in Time

**Lisa's short stories:**
<u>Chartreuse</u>
<u>The Angst of Change</u>
<u>BAAC</u>
<u>Melting</u>
<u>Armsby</u>

Lisa's 31-book mini mystery series set in Salem Massachusetts begins with:
<u>The Lucky Cat – Black Cat Vol. 1</u>

Here are a few of Lisa's self-help books:

<u>Secrets to Falling Asleep</u>
Get Better Sleep to Improve Health and Reduce Stress

<u>Dream Symbol Encyclopedia</u>
Interpretation and Meaning of Dream Symbols

<u>Lucid Dreaming Guide</u>
Foster Creativity in a Lucid Dream State

<u>Learning to say NO – and YES! To your Dream</u>
Protect your goals while gently helping others succeed

<u>Reduce Stress Instantly</u>
Practical relaxation tips you can use right now for instant stress relief

<u>Time Management Course</u>
Learn to End Procrastination, Increase Productivity, and Reduce Stress

<u>Simple Ways to Make the World Better for Everyone</u>
Every day we wake up is a day to take a fresh path, to help a friend, and to improve our lives.

Author's proceeds from all these books benefit battered women's shelters.

"Be the change you wish to see in the world."

CPSIA information can be obtained at www.ICGtesting.com
Printed in the USA
LVOW06s1428251015

459660LV00001B/61/P

9 781507 744093